John Almon

A Letter to the Right Honourable Charles Jenkinson

John Almon

A Letter to the Right Honourable Charles Jenkinson

ISBN/EAN: 9783337195717

Printed in Europe, USA, Canada, Australia, Japan

Cover: Foto ©Andreas Hilbeck / pixelio.de

More available books at **www.hansebooks.com**

A

L E T T E R

TO THE RIGHT HONOURABLE

CHARLES JENKINSON.

THE SECOND EDITION.

L O N D O N:

Printed for J. DEBRETT (Succeſſor to Mr. Almon) oppoſite
Burlington Houſe, in Piccadilly. 1781.

A

L E T T E R

TO THE

Right Hon. CHARLES JENKINSON.

S I R,

THE fphere in which you move, and the part which you take, in the government of this country, render any apology for this addrefs totally unneceffary. The furprife, if it occafions any, fhould not be at the thing itfelf, but that public addreffes to you have not been made before, and often. Men of lefs importance in the ftate, have been brought before the tribunal of the public, their conduct has been examined with freedom, and cenfured with fpirit, for meafures over which they have had lefs influence than you have over our public councils. How you have efcaped, I fhall not at prefent give myfelf much trouble to explain; though, were I to indulge in that theme, I fhould afcribe it to your early knowledge of the management of the prefs.

If I miftake not, you were efteemed an ufeful typographical *commis* at the Oxfordfhire election, in the year 1754; when you inked your virgin pen in fupport of the Whig intereft. A dinner at the late Lord Harcourt's fecond table, was not unufual. And when his Lordfhip and his friends had dined, you were fometimes called in; and from the converfation of the company, and being a young man of pliable notions, you received, with a never-failing bending acquiefcence, thofe hints which you afterwards worked up for the prefs.

Early habits are not soon worn off; the *Cacoethes Scribendi* laid the foundation of your present opulence. I believe, Sir, that you are the first writer who can boast of such ample rewards! Mr. Addison, with his evidences *for*, and Mr. Gibbon with his evidences *against*, the Christian religion, met with none such. And Mr. Burke, whose genius, judgment, and knowledge, all descriptions of men will allow, yield to none of the present age, compared to you, has been but a bungler in worldly pursuits. He has written for general use—you for your own. The *temporary* object, and not the *principle* of the thing, always directed your attention, and guided your pen. Accordingly, in a short period after the Oxfordshire election, we saw you supporting, I mean with your pen, the Whig administration of the late Duke of Newcastle.

When the great minister of that day, ordered those Dutch trading vessels to be taken, which were carrying assistance to the enemy, you wrote a pamphlet, entitled, *A Discourse on the Conduct of the Government of Great Britain in respect to Neutral Nations*; approving to the extent, and defending to the utmost, those captures. Lord Harcourt finding you "on all occasions apt," but knowing that Mr. Pitt trusted as little to the press for the applause due to his conduct, as he did to parliament for the approbation of it; his Lordship took you to his friend, the late Mr. Grenville, then Treasurer of the Navy; to whom he kindly and cordially recommended you, as deserving of something, for writing the pamphlet; and who might, in that line, (for Lord Harcourt never meant more) be useful to government. Mr. Grenville, at his Lordship's request, mentioned the matter to the Duke of Newcastle. The old Whig had a great deal of the milk of human kindness in his nature; but there being at that time no little *fine cure* vacant, he gave you a pension of two hundred pounds per annum; which, I am informed, you still continue to receive.

From

From this sketch of your juvenile performances, I wish to make a short digression, respecting the present day. Having been accustomed to see my country in the zenith of glory, under the guidance of that great minister whose magnanimity you industriously vindicated in the above-mentioned pamphlet, I lament, in tears, her fallen condition; under a *new* system of *secret* and *unresponsible influence*: Nor is it with any abatement of the same sorrow, that I likewise lament, that you did not take with you into power, the *principle* and *opinions* of that great minister, with regard to Holland; the very point on which you had defended him. The councils of his present Majesty, having by a barbarous wantonness, added the enmity of nation to nation against us, the accumulation of Holland (to speak of it in the mildest terms) was impolitic, unnecessary, and unnatural. Mr. Pitt seized the Dutch merchantmen, it is true, but he did not go to war with the State. He was too great a politician, not to know the *error*, or as he would have called it, the *insanity* of such a war. His administration was stained by no *puerile* passions.

Upon your introduction into the Secretary's office, under Lord Holdernesse, no matter whether by the solicitation of your mother, who was a domestic in his Lordship's family, or any other solicitation, is not material; we do not find by the red book, that his Lordship esteemed your abilities equal to those of an ordinary clerk, on the establishment; for we saw you in the office, only as a *supernumerary*. It does not appear that you had the least connection with Mr. Pitt's office. That great man was rarely deceived in his subalterns; he chose for himself. But when Lord Bute succeeded Lord Holdernesse, we saw you taken *into confidence*; and when his Lordship stepped into the Treasury, he took you in his hand. · It was said at the time, that Mr. Samuel Martin and yourself (both under the greatest obligations to the Duke of Newcastle and the Whigs) were his Lordship's *miners,*

in

in that memorable explosion of the Whig interest, which began with the dismission of Mr. Legge.

Your adroitness in rescuing Lord Bute from the distress and difficulties into which his own indiscretion and precipitate promises to the city of London had plunged him, in the affair of the excise upon cyder, gained you the interest and confidence of the closet. We know the press was managed at that time; but it was not till afterwards, that your interviews with the late Sir James Hodges, upon the business, were known; nor that you had, by Lord Bute's specific direction, entered into a negotiation with Sir James, after one had failed which had been attempted by the late Sir John Philips.

It is not worth while to illustrate your rise and influence by any more facts. One sentence is sufficient for all the rest, which is, though Lord Bute has retired, you are, in the city phrase, his *locum tenens*. You are the favourite of the present day, " that sokes up the King's " countenance, his rewards, his authorities; but such officers do the " King best service in the end; he keeps them like an apple in the " corner of his jaw; first mouthed to be last swallowed: when he " needs what you have gleaned, it is but squeezing you, and, spunge, " you shall be dry again."

The confidence you now enjoy of your sovereign, and the possession you hold of his ear, make it highly necessary, and it is no less constitutional, that you should be known to your country. It is for this reason that I have done myself the honour of addressing this public letter to you. Though not a first rate minister by your office, yet more than either Walpole or Pitt in the closet. I mean the interior closet. They were ministers in the official closet. In the present reign, there has been another closet added: one is the closet of business, the other of form.

The Earl of Mansfield's distinction, in the House of Lords, gave us the purest and truest idea of the *situation*, and *division* of the members.

bers.

bers of both closets. One his Lordship denominated the *Efficient* Coun-cil, the other, the *Official* Council. Whatever might have been our suspicions before that time, and we were not without suspicions, yet we had neither the authority, nor ability, to ascertain the distinction so *precisely* and *happily* as his Lordship.

It is a public loss that the noble Earl, when he so concisely and ex-actly pointed the distinction in the royal councils, that he did not, at the same time, name, as well as describe the parties.

His Lordship could have told us, whether the reports were true.—That the efficient council meet, in conclave, at a certain house in Stable Yard.—That the Falkland Island business was not communicated to the *official*, until the *efficient* (under the auspices of Mr. Stuart Mackenzie) had settled it.—That the late Lord Clive was condemned by the *official*, but saved by the *efficient*.—That Lord North's propo-sitions in 1777, for peace with America, was settled by the *official*, but totally changed by the *efficient*.—That upon his next proposition in 1778, he threatened to resign if that was altered, therefore he was allowed to have the honour to bring *his own* propositions to parliament that year; but the *efficient men* altered it there, by throwing the whole measure into the hands of the Crown, and afterwards they changed Mr. Jackson, whom the official ministers had appointed one of the Commissioners, he being a more capable and proper person than any of those who went, and put in Mr. Governor Commodore John-stone, who knew less of the business than Lord Carlisle.—That upon the delivery of the Rescript from the Court of Spain, his Majesty called his *official* ministers to a long table, in the Queen's Palace, and there delivered to them a long speech,* declaring his resolution to carry on the war against America, France, and Spain; and they whispered to one another, *who has made all this for him?* thereby admitting, to the fullest extent, the fact of an *all-powerful* and *invisible* agency.—That

C   an

---

* You are said to have been the writer of this most singular literary curiosity. It was too precious a morsel to be trusted with the Infidel of the Board of Trade.

an attempt was made, a few days before the delivery of the Rescript, to open a negotiation for a peace with America, upon terms which, at least for the purpose of *beginning*, had the approbation of some of the *official* ministers, but were decided against by the *efficient* council.

I could proceed until I had tired the reader, in stating (though briefly) the many other reports of pretended facts, of the like *extraordinary complexion*; in all which, the noble Earl could, with his happy facility and precision, have marked the distinction of truth. and falsehood. The future historian, (for a third historian may arise if Dr. Robertson and Mr. Gibbon should die) would have given to his memory, the sweet incense of gratitude; for who, like him, can

———— make the worse appear
The better reason.

The official ministers are always known. They are always to be found in the red book of every year. But the efficient counsellors are not so well known. The only reason I have heard given for this secrecy is, the extreme nicety and importance of their stations; both of which it is said are beyond the conception of vulgar understanding. Sometimes we think we can guess at them pretty exactly, but upon some occasions even the official ministers have their doubts. Like Jupiter's satellites, or the Mogul's nabobs, they frequently eclipse each other.

However, among the foremost of this efficient group, we have the satisfaction of being certain, you are never omitted;—except during your amorous dalliance after Miss A. It was no doubt ludicrous to see a tall thin old man of 54, over head and ears in love with a girl of 18. But you were soon brought back to your duty, by the sage advice, and grave deportment of your brother, " the able and impartial Speaker ;" who " lacking advancement," and knowing your all-powerful influence in the interior closet, lost no time in reclaiming the truant boy. He judged right ; for in the next Parliament, you made him Speaker.

It is, Sir, in your present situation as foremost, or deputy to the foremost of the efficient council, that I have the honour to address myself

to

to you. Whether such a situation is strictly constitutional, the learned Doctors in his Majesty's service, may explain and expound as they please; or what is more probable, according to their interest; but I, who was early taught in the old Whig school, the common law, and the old Constitution, can see no legality, can discover no constitutional authority, whereon is grounded this *arcanum imperii*, this state of privity behind a privy council.

The parliament are the constitutional advisers of the King; by them the King acts with the concurrence and support of the people; but because parliament cannot be always convened, nor be always kept sitting, the King is allowed to chose himself a private council (*id est*, the privy council); but these private counsellors, being instruments of delegation, are answerable to parliament for the advice they give from time to time, to the King. *

The ministers of the present reign, who, with very few exceptions, have been uniform Tories, admit, by their conduct, the force and justice of this Whig principle. But by a new and cunning inversion of things, they make parliament the executive power in the first instance; and then take their intended measures, under the authority of an act of parliament.

Whatever measures are resolved upon by the efficient council, with respect to America, Asia, &c. the official ministers begin the work with

---

* Formerly all matters of state and discretion were debated and resolved in the privy council. Charles the Second was the first who broke this excellent part of our constitution, by settling a CABAL where all matters of consequence were debated and resolved, and then brought to the privy council to be confirmed. The first footsteps we have of this council in any European government were in Charles the Ninth's time in France, when resolving to massacre the Protestants, he durst not trust his council with it, but chose a few men whom he called his cabinet council; and considering what a genealogy it had, it is no wonder it has been so fatal both to King and people. For whatever miscarriages there are, nobody can be punished for them, for they justify themselves by a sign manual, or perhaps a private direction from the King."

Mr. Trenchard's Preface to the History of Standing Armies.

an act of parliament. Inſtead of adviſing meaſures, in the firſt in-
ſtance, they act under an act of parliament. They ſend fleets and
armies, to enforce an act of parliament.

The Stuart Kings attempted to govern without a parliament; but
the Whigs of thoſe days complained of the innovation, and corrected
the abuſe. In our time, the principle is reverſed. It is determined
to puniſh the Whigs every way; therefore ſo far from having too little
of parliament, you have reſolved we ſhall have too much. Parliament
are not only the makers, but the executors of the law; and the miniſters are ſimply no more, than the ſheriffs in the buſineſs, giving
orders to their officers and conſtables.

The meaſure which ſquanders millions of pounds, and ſacrifices
thouſands of lives, ſecretly originates in an efficient council. It is
next, by ſome deputed member, or by a higher authority, communicated to the official miniſters. They are obliged to adopt it, for that
is the tenure by which they hold their offices. But then theſe official
miniſters, to evade the conſtitutional reſponſibility of their ſitua-
tions, move in parliament for leave to bring in a bill; and, by a
happy influence over parliament, the bill is paſſed. The miniſters thus
conſider themſelves juſtified in their conduct, having the authority of
parliament on their ſide; for an act of parliament thus obtained,
operates to them, as an act of indemnity.

To this new principle and new practice in our politics, we muſt
aſcribe all our misfortunes. Miniſters durſt not have proceeded with
ſuch alacrity in the execution of meaſures, (which are ſuppoſed to
have originated with perſons, in no reſponſible offices) if thoſe meaſures had not firſt been authorized by an act of parliament. They
would not have begun a war with America (though the reſolution for
war had been taken by the efficient council long before the action
at Lexington) without firſt having " the law on their ſide " Nor
have afterwards given up the *pretended* cauſe of diſpute, without again
havin

ing " the law on their fide." The enemy need not be at the expence of spies, for they may always know what measures are intended by the bills which are passing. Facts and dates will state
this matter better than a thousand arguments.

In the month of December, 1777, Lord North twice mentioned in
the House of Commons the wishes of the King's servants to " con-
ciliate" with America. On the 11th of February, 1778, he promised to
bring in his plan of conciliation in a few days. On the 17th, he brought
in his two bills, for appointing Commissioners, and removing doubts.
They received the royal assent on the 11th of March —On the 6th
of February, 1778, the treaty between France and America was signed
at Paris. And on the 23d of March, 1778, the same Lord North brought
a message from his Majesty, informing the House of the French treaty.
A treaty which effectually defeated, in every shape, all the promised
good effects of the two bills, passed but a few days before. But the mis-
chief does not end here. The Dutch war, takes its rise from the same
caution in the minister, not stirring, until he has an act of parliament
on his side. It appears from De Neufville's letter to Dr. Franklin (which
letter was not laid before parliament, though it ought to have been,
however it is to be found in the *Remembrancer*, together with many
more valuable papers) dated in July, 1779, that De Neufville had his
interview a twelvemonth before, with Mr. William Lee, at Aix-la-
Chapelle, upon the eventual treaty, between Holland and America.
Lee must have had his instructions from the Congress. The time
between the *bringing in* the bills, and this interview, is fully sufficient
for a voyage from Europe to America, and back. From these premises, it is a fair and just conclusion, that Holland, as well as France,
seeing the possibility of a re-union between Great Britain and America,
agreed to the proposals of the American ministers.

The sanguinary act of hiring foreign troops, produced the declaration of Independence, together with the first applications from Ame-

D

rica

rica for affiftance to the Courts in Europe. The conciliatory bills as they were falfely called, produced a triple war, with France, Spain, and Holland.

If thefe dates and facts are indifputable, and I believe they are, the inference to be drawn from them need not be fuggefted. Every man will reafon for himfelf, and whether he chufes to confefs it, or not, he muft in his own private judgment condemn the efficient council, and the official minifters. There is not an epithet of reproach in the language fit for one man to ufe to another, which they have not deferved: by fuperlative ignorance in affecting to plan, and by treacherous impotence in affuming to execute.

I remember to have heard (and I am within the memory of many gentlemen, who heard you as well as myfelf) you fay in parliament, that the ftamp act did not originate with Mr. Grenville; it was recommended to him, and he adopted it.—It was candid to do juftice to his memory. Whatever his miftakes might be, and every man has made fome miftakes, he certainly meant well to this country. But your candid acknowledgment admits, by implication, that the efficient council exifted in his time; and if I remember right, Mr. Scott, in his letters figned Anti-Sejanus, pofitively afferted that the influence of the Earl of Bute, though himfelf out of all office, was yet as full, and abfolute, over every department of the ftate, as when he *openly* held the reins of Government.

This order of an efficient council, though inftituted fince the year 1761, does not feem to have been crudely defigned, nor directed to any particular object. For if a judgment may be formed upon public facts, it may fafely be affirmed, that this dark, unfeen, unknown, and unrefponfible council has been eftablifhed, with a view to controul and manage the whole machine of government of this country and all her dependencies; to unite every thing in one central focus, and to make that focus the Crown. That it has been the uniform, fet-
tled:

tled fyftem of the clofet (the only fyftem that has been settled and perfevered in) fince the acceffion of the Earl of Bute.

There is another fact that is more to be lamented than all the reft; that requires our contrition and forrow, more than any circumftance in the hiftory of thefe times. The *nominal* minifter's anfwer to a private application from a fmall number of the India Directors, (no doubt given precipitately and unwarily) contains the *true* caufe of the unhappy war with America; and places it nearer to the clofet, than any good fubject wifhed to have difcovered it. It was pretended by the miniftry, that the American tea duty was left ftanding, when the duties on paint, glafs, &c. were repealed, in order to give a bonus to the Eaft India Company. The affertion was totally untrue. The tea fent to Bofton was Bohea, which was no burden to the Company. It was the Singlo that was on hand, and in all the Company's warehoufes. Therefore the tea fent to America, was not the *fort* of tea to ferve the Company. This was explained to the miniftry. However, the refolution was carried in a private committee of *three* only. Mr. Bolton was chairman. Such a meafure ought to have been agitated in a *full* committee, which is eleven. The matter was afterwards objected to at the minifter's houfe, when his Lordfhip haftily faid, *it was, to no purpofe making objections, for the —— would have it fo*; thofe were his Lordfhip's words, and he added, *that the —— meant to try the queftion with America.*

The proceedings in one part of America, (and one part was fufficient) were perfectly correfpondent. The tea was deftroyed at Bofton. A few facts feem almoft to warrant the affertion, that the whole purpofe of the law was completely anfwered by the deftruction of the tea. At other ports, the veffels laden with tea, were fent back. At Bofton they were not. The Governor (the tea was configned to his fon) refufed to permit the veffels to return, without a clearance. The Captains could not get a clearance from the Cuftom-Houfe, becaufe unaffifted,

affifted, and unprotected, they could not land their cargoes. If the Governor had ordered the tea to be put into the men of war's barges, then lying there, and each barge to have been armed with a few marines, the whole tea might have been fafely lodged in the King's warehoufes, under the efcort of the marines; or the Governor might, if he had thought proper, have permitted the veffels to fail, without breaking bulk, as was done at the other ports in America. But he would neither affift the Captains to land the tea, nor fuffer the fhips to return, until they had, fome way or other, got rid of their cargoes.

It is a pity we cannot do juftice to the great abilities, which fo ably contrived this whole meafure. The conftitution has not given us a channel to afcertain and identify the contrivers. The whole merit of it feems to belong to the efficient council—or—perhaps to yourfelf.

This refinement in our conftitution, of making the law *precede* the provocation; and of creating, under the law, thofe tranfactions which are to be punifhed according to law; excels every artifice we read of in the reigns of the Stuarts. It was not provided againft, at either the reftoration, or revolution, becaufe fuch a manœuvre was not thought of. The immaculate wifdom of an efficient council, ftruck out this new light.

It is the argument of lawyers, that in every ftate there muft be a *dernier power* fomewhere. The *efficient* council owes its inftitution to this doctrine. But it is a dangerous doctrine, for it makes the conftitution warrant an *invifible* power; whereas our government is a *truft* from the people, and fomebody muft be *anfwerable* for the *exercife* of every part of it. There is a claufe in the act of fettlement, which directs, that every privy counfellor fhall fign his name to the advice he gives his Sovereign. It is a misfortune, that this claufe is not better obferved. The framers of the act of fettlement, judged, in the true fpirit of the conftitution, that all the functions of government being but fo many *commiffions* of *delegation*, the people for whofe happinefs

pines all government is inftituted, have a right to know the *authors*
and *advifers* of every meafure, accepted, adopted, or taken by the
crown ; for as the crown can do nothing but by advice, the furest way
of knowing the advifer, was to oblige him to fign his name to the advice he gave. *Hic murus aheneus efto.*

Sir Fletcher Norton, in one of his pleadings on the fide of general
warrants, in the Court of Common Pleas, having laid down this doctrine of a dernier power, Lord Chief Juftice Pratt, now Lord Camden, with great energy and perfpicuity, replied, that if he underftood
the conftitutional idea of a dernier power, it belonged to cafes of appeal : it was the *laft* decifion, no matter where, nor by whom.
Queftions of no kind could originate in a dernier power ; they might
end, but could not begin in one.

Admitting, for the novelty, that the efficient council could juftify
its inftitution, from the law-arguments, in fupport of a dernier power,
and not to fay any thing of the impeachment thereby made of the wifdom of parliament, and of the King's privy council, there would ftill a
very formidable queftion arife, on the *extent* of the power claimed.
It is poffible, that a minifter, like Lord Chatham, might not chufe to
be dictated to ; or, that like fome others, he might accept of the dic-
tation confined to certain limits : In any cafe, a refiftance by the *official*
council muft occafion great confufion, and throw the whole ma-
chinery of the interior clofet into a heap of ruins ; which circumftance
happened when Mr. Grenville went out in 1765. For this *efficient*
council lives not by the authority of minifters, but by their acquiefcence ; and while minifters can be found, who will proftitute their
names, their characters, and their talents, in this fervile, fecond-rate
degree, this *efficient* council will exift, and no longer.

Now let us view, for a moment only, to what danger does this innovation in our conftitution lead. It affumes to pervade, not only
all executive government, but all legiflative and judicial authority ; all

E   civil

civil and military power, as well as regulation. It ufurps a general, fweeping, arbitrary domination, from which no man is fafe, no property exempt. No means of redrefs can be inftituted againft it, becaufe it is cognizable no where. It is a Leviathan and a non-entity; an invifible hydra; a phœnix rifing out of the afhes of the old inquifition, or rather (to drop all figure) from being a government according to law, this *new power* makes it a government according to difcretion, without refponfibility in the advifers.

At the time of the Spanifh war with the Netherlands the Duke of Alva had a council, which was denominated *the Council of Blood.* I believe none of the hiftorians give us a lift of that council. But Philip loft the Netherlands, by purfuing the meafures and advice of that council. *

Philip

---

* There is fuch a ftrong analogy, between the war with the Netherlands, and the war with America, that for the reader's entertainment, I will extract a few traits, chiefly from the works of Sir William Temple.

" The Emperor Charles the Fifth, left to his fon Philip, the Seventeen Provinces in the Low Countries, as peaceable and as loyal as either prince or fubjects could defire. Philip coming to the poffeffion, of fo many and great dominions, after the trial of fortune in the war with France (which was left him by his father like an incumbrance upon an eftate) reftored by the peace of Cambray the quiet of all his dominions. After this he went into Spain, leaving the Spanifh and Italian troops in the Low Countries, with the fame demands of fupplies from the States which the war had made neceffary. By this conduct he foon ceafed to be loved, and began to be feared by the inhabitants of thofe provinces. He conferred the offices of his houfe and the honour of his council and confidence upon Spaniards, whofe refervednefs and pride were difagreeable to the Flemings. But Philip thought it not agreeing with the pomp and greatnefs of the Houfe of Auftria, nor with his defigns of a great empire, to confider the grievances of the Low Countries, nor to be limited by their ancient forms of government. He had agreed with the Pope to eftablifh fourteen new Bifhops in the Low Countries, and he refolved to revive the edicts againft Luther, to make way for the inquifition.

" The erecting of fourteen new bifhops fees, was looked upon by the great Lords as an innovation, by introducing fo many new men into the great council. Vol. I. p. 77. Count Egmont was fent to Spain to reprefent the grievances of the provinces to the King, who difpatched him back with a favourable anfwer, by which the rigors of the edicts and inquifition were remitted. But in a very fhort time he fent letters to the

Duchefs

Philip had as many opportunities of making peace with the Netherlands, as you have had with America. But his *Council of Blood* were
always for another campaign. The hiftorians of thofe times fay, that
they

Duchefs of Parma, Governefs of the Low Countries, difclaiming the interpretation
given to his letters by Count Egmont, and declaring that his will was, all heretics fhould
be put to death, and the edicts fhould be publifhed and obferved.

" This occafioned a confederacy of the Lords never to fuffer the inquifition in the
Low Countries, as contrary to all laws, both facred and profane ; executions were prevented, prifons forced open, &c.

" Brederode at the head of two hundred gentlemen, petitioned the Governefs at
Bruffels to abolifh the inquifition and edicts concerning religion. She fent the petition to the King ; but though the King was ftartled with fuch confequences of his laft
commands, and at length induced to recall them ; yet whether by the flownefs of his
nature, or the forms of the Court, the anfwer came too late ; and as all his former con-
ceffions, either by delay, or teftimonies of ill-will, or meaning in them, had loft the
good grace, fo this loft abfolutely the effect, and came into the Low Countries when
all was in a flame. P. 81.

" In 1567, the Duke of Alva arrived at Bruffels, with an army of 10,000, the beft
Spanifh and Italian foldiers, under the command of the choiceft officers, which the wars
of Charles V. and Philip II. had bred up in Europe, which, with 2000 Germans raifed
by the Dutchefs of Parma, made up a force, which nothing in the Low Countries could
look in the face, with other eyes than of aftonifhment, fubmiffion, or defpair. P. 83.

" The Duke of Alva was vefted with powers never given before to any Governor ; a
council of twelve was erected for trial of all crimes committed againft the King's authority, which was called by the people the Council of Blood. Great numbers were
condemned and executed by fentence of this council. The town ftomached the breach
of their charters, and the people of their liberties, and all complain of the difufe of the
ftates, and of the introduction of armies ; but all in vain. The King was conftant to
what he had determined." P. 84.

Alva demanded new taxes for his troops, the people refufed to pay them, he threatened to hang them.—Sir W. Temple's words are thefe.

" The people refufe to pay, the foldiers begin to levy by force, the townfmen all fhut
up their fhops, the people in the country forbear the market. The Duke is enraged, and
calls the foldiers to arms, and commands feveral of the inhabitants who refufed the
payments, to be hanged that very night upon their fign pofts ; which nothing moves
the obftinacy of the people : and now the officers of the guards are ready to begin the
executions, when news comes to town of the taking of the Briel, (by the perfons who
accompanied Brederode, when he delivered the petition to the Duchefs of Parma) and
of the expectation that had been given of a fudden revolt in the province of Holland.

" This

ley entertained great hopes of getting large confiscated estates, particularly the Prince of Orange's, &c. When the Dutch applied to England and France for assistance—When Philip recalled the Duke of Alva,

" This unexpected blow struck the Duke of Alva, and foreseeing the consequence of it, because he knew the stubble was dry; and now he found the fire was fallen in, he thought it an ill time to make an end of the tragedy in Brabant, whilst a new scene was opened in Holland; and so giving over for the present his taxes and executions, applies his thoughts to the suppression of this new enemy. Thus began the second great commotion of the Low-Countries in 1570, and that which, indeed, never ended, but in the loss of those provinces, where the death of the Spanish and royal government gave life to a new Commonwealth." P. 87.

How similar is this to the American war! TAXES form the cause, or rather the pretence for both wars. So true it is, that the same oppression will create the same opposition, or, in the common phrase, the same cause will produce the same effect.

The war raged with various success. The surprise of Briel and the surprise of Trenton were not unlike in their consequences, except that the former " proved to Philip a dear experience; how little the best conduct and boldest armies are able to withstand the torrent of an enraged people, which ever bears down all before it." P. 91.

Fresh armies and new commanders were sent. Don John of Austria succeeded the Duke of Alva. The Duke of Parma succeeded Don John. This duke was to annihilate all resistance. The States prepared for him, and the union of Utrecht in 1579 was made upon his coming. The Archduke Albert succeeded the Duke of Parma, he came also with a mighty army, drawn out of Germany and Italy.

" The Spanish and Italian writers, says Sir William Temple, content themselves to attribute the cause of this revolution to the change of religion, to the native stubbornness of the people, and to the ambition of the Prince of Orange; but religion, without mixture of ambition and interest, works no such violent effects, and produces rather the examples of constant sufferings, than of desperate actions. The nature of the people cannot change of a sudden, no more than the climate which infuses it; and no country hath brought forth better subjects than many of these provinces, both before and since these commotions; and the ambition of one man could neither have designed nor atchieved so great an adventure, had it not been seconded with universal discontent; nor could that have been raised to so great an height and heat, without so many circumstances, as fell in from an unhappy course of the Spanish Counsels to kindle, and foment it. P. 96.

" The continuance of foreign troops after the wars begun by Charles V. were ended; the erecting of the new bishop's sees, and introducing the inquisition, and the imposition of the 10th and 20th part against the legal forms of government, in a country where a long derived succession had made the people fond and tenacious of their

antient

Alva, and Don John of Auſtria acceded to the engagement of Ghent
—When the Prince of Orange was aſſaſſinated at Delph—When the
perfidy of Leiceſter had nearly ſacrificed the Dutch—and upon ſeveral
other

antient cuſtoms and laws. Theſe were the ſeeds of their hatred to Spain, which were
encreaſed by the courſe of above threeſcore years war. P. 97.

" The choice of the Archduke Albert had a deeper root and deſign than at firſt
appeared ; for that mighty King Philip II. born to ſo vaſt poſſeſſions, and to ſo much
vaſter deſires, after a long dream of raiſing his head into the clouds, found it now
ready to lie down in the duſt ; his body broken with age and infirmities, his mind with
cares and diſtempered thoughts, and the royal ſervitude of a ſoliſitous life, he began
to ſee in the glaſs of time and experience, the true ſhapes of all human greatneſs and
deſigns ; and finding to what airy figures he had hitherto ſacrificed his health and caſe and
the good of his life, he now turned his thoughts wholly to reſt and quiet, which he had
never yet allowed either the world or himſelf. His deſigns upon England, and his in-
vincible armada had ended in ſmoke ; thoſe upon France, in events the moſt contrary
to what he had propoſed : and inſtead of maſtering the liberties, and breaking the
ſtomach of his Low-Country ſubjects, he had loſt ſeven of his provinces, and held
the reſt by the tenure of a war that coſt more than they were worth. He had lately
made a peace with England, and deſired it with France ; and though he ſcorned it
with his revolted ſubjects in his own name, yet he wiſhed it in another's, and was
unwilling to entail a quarrel upon his ſon, which had croſſed his fortunes, and buſied
his thoughts all the courſe of his reign ; he therefore reſolved to commit theſe two
deſigns to the management of Archduke Albert, with the ſtile of Governor and
Prince of the Low-Countries, to the end that if he could reduce the provinces to
their old ſubjection, he ſhould govern them as Spaniſh dominions ; if that was in
vain, he ſhould, by a marriage with Clara Iſabella Eugenia, (King Philip's beloved
daughter) receive theſe provinces as a dowry, and become Prince of them, with a
condition only of their returning to Spain, in caſe of Iſabella dying without iſſue ; and
at the worſt, King Philip thought they might make a peace without affecting the honour of the Spaniſh Crown.

" The Archduke entered the Low-Countries with a large army, but like all the
former, it was of no effect. The Dutch had opened veins of trade with ſeveral nations, and both the Indies, and from theſe they derived thoſe great reſources, which
enabled them to ſtand againſt their powerful enemy. At length, Albert propoſed a
truce ; the very mention of it, ſays Sir William Temple, could hardly at firſt be
faſtened upon the States, nor could they ever be prevailed upon to make way for

F

any

other occasions Philip might have made peace, but the false pride of royalty would not let him ask it, though being the aggressor, he ought to have offered it. The States felt their own magnanimity, and recovered themselves.

In the year 1777, America was more than once on the point of breaking with France—she was disappointed in not receiving the assistance which France had promised her, this was our time to have stepped in, and separated them totally; or if Lord Percy had gone to America, at the time it was proposed to have sent him, with the powers then pretended to be in contemplation, such a separation might have been accomplished, and it is probable we might have made peace with America: at least, a separation from France at that time would have led very essentially towards it; but after an establishment of secretaries, clerks, &c. was agreed upon, the negotiation with Lord Percy broke off as abruptly as it had begun. His Lordship asked no emolument, only an honorary mark of distinction—a blue ribband. The ostensible Minister, who has so often declared his sorrow for the American war, and his readiness to make peace, would not give it him, though there were three blue ribbands at that time vacant, viz. Lord Albemarle's, Lord Chesterfield's, and the Duke of Kingston's, but *promised* him he should have it when he returned. Lord Percy replied, he was too well acquainted with Courts to trust to *promises*, and if he could not have it before he went, he must decline going.*

A few

any negotiation by a suspension of arms, till the Archduke had declared, he would treat with them as free provinces, upon whom neither he nor Spain had any pretence. The truce was signed in 1609, and thus the state of the United Provinces came to be acknowledged as a free Commonwealth by their antient master, having before been treated so by most of the Kings and Princes of Europe." P. 110.

* The supposition of the world has been, that the Efficient Council were not friendly to the intended embassy of Lord Percy, and that when Lord North made
the

(23)

A few months afterwards, another opportunity offered of opening a negotiation with America, before the treaty with France was signed. This was by Monſ Thornton, who came avowedly commiſſioned by Dr. Franklin and Mr. Deane to open a negotiation with the Miniſtry reſpecting the American priſoners, particularly thoſe in England. He waited upon Lord North ſeveral times in the month of December, 1777, to whom he delivered a letter from the American Miniſter. He was in London three weeks, by the knowledge of government, yet neither the *efficient* Council, nor the *official* Miniſters ever offered to open a treaty through him with Dr. Franklin, notwithſtanding the opportunity was ſo fair and inviting. In about four weeks after his return to Paris, the treaty between France and America was ſigned.

The attempts made by Lord Chatham, Mr. Burke, General Conway, Mr. Hartley, and many other gentlemen, form a group of circumſtantial evidence, that peace with America was never intended, until, as Lord Nord ſaid, ſhe was brought to our feet; or, as Lord George Germaine expreſſed himſelf, ſhe had made unconditional ſubmiſſion.

When you reſolved upon making war with America, and that nothing ſhort of abſolute conqueſt was to put an end to it, you ſhould at the ſame time have formed your plan for European policy. You ſhould have had a ſyſtem. You ſhould have had ſome great ally on the continent of Europe. It was obvious to every man, that a civil war in the Britiſh empire muſt be an invitation to France to revenge the loſſes and diſgraces ſhe ſuffered in the laſt war. A powerful ally upon the continent might have kept her in check.

The *efficient* Council of his preſent Majeſty, have been the firſt Council ſince the revolution who have diſregarded the wiſe policy of preſerving the balance of power. Great Britain joined to America

was

the requeſt of the blue ribband known to his maſter, they refuſed it, in order to put an end to the deſign.

was a balance againſt all the Roman Catholic States in Europe. It was America that turned the ſcale ſo triumphantly in our favour throughout the laſt war. The peace of 1761, made a new æra in the ſyſtem, but no deviation from the principle of it; though we did not gain all that we had a right to expect, yet America was gained, and ſhe, alone, was a balance of power in our favour. The old ſyſtem of King William had been continued, protected, and cheriſhed in the growth and acquiſition of the new nation of America; while we had her immenſe trade in our ports, and her encreaſing ſtrength on our ſide; it would have been indifferent to theſe kingdoms, whether Charles or Philip ſat on the throne of Spain, or the Elector of Bavaria, or the Queen of Hungary, ſucceeded to the Imperial diadem.

Whoever adviſed that fatal reſolution of *trying* the queſtion with America, was a ſhallow, as well as a wicked politician. It was obvious, that America diſmembered, though but for a time, muſt be ſuch diminution of our ſtrength, that no man, who was fit to be a Miniſter, would have commenced hoſtilities with America, without firſt having gained the eventual acceſſion, at leaſt, of a contingent ſtrength in Europe, in caſe of France aſſiſting America; a ſuppoſition, that muſt occur to the plaineſt underſtanding.

If Lord Chatham had choſen to have made war upon America, he would have had an ally in Europe; he would have added ſtrength to the body, before he had attempted to coerce the extremities; but he knew the neceſſity of preſerving the great political outline of former days, the balance of power, and he never ſuffered it to eſcape his eye for a moment. He knew that America was that balance of power to England; that ſhe was arrived at ſuch ſtate of perfection and maturity, that England with America in her hand, might treat with a contemptuous ſmile the frowns of every Prince in Europe. She was

that

that accession of encreasing strength and wealth, that unsubsidized auxillary, whose faith was guarantied by blood, interest, laws, language, manners, and religion, all the strongest ties which bind the hearts and passions of men; and therefore he was so zealous and warm, against the dismemberment of the Empire. But were he now alive, he could not prevent America becoming a separate nation. All opportunities of peace, all hopes of accommodation, without the preliminary of Independence, are totally lost. Whenever peace is made, we shall then feel our loss of him most sensibly.

He could have done something with America, though not all he wished. But those ministers, who have had the management of the war, and have been beat by the Americans, both in field and in council, can never make a good peace. America must detest them for their cruelties, and repeated acts of duplicity. And the ministers of the belligerant powers in Europe, must hold them in too light an estimation, for any negotiation, except the surface of a convenient truce, whenever those powers shall condescend to listen to it.

Will Lord George Germain come forward and tell us he understands peace better than war. He cannot have the effrontery; though from the specimens he has given us, of his knowledge in both sciences, his competency to either, may be well disputed. If the other ministers were applied to, upon the same subject, would they not officially answer, that the cause of the war having originated in his Lordship's department, the preliminary and ultimatum of peace, being the Independence of America, must come from the same place? His Lordship's prowess in war, is upon record;—his skill in peace, is known in America, though not in England: however, it may be seen in his letter to Sir Henry Clinton and Admiral Arbuthnot, sent by the New-York packet in March last; which was taken, and his Lordship's letter published in Philadelphia, with Annotations.

G ·   *Whitehall,*

Whitehall, 7th March, 1781.

" Gentlemen,

" I HAVE received your difpatch of the 2d of January, and one from Sir Henry Clinton of the 20th; and had the honour to lay them before the King.

" Your declaration of the 29th December, inclofed in your joint difpatch, will, I truft, be productive of all the good effects you hope from it, and which fo well timed a publication intitles you to expect, and I fhall be very happy to carry to the King an application to you from any of the revolted Provinces for pardon, and reftoration to the privileges of Britifh fubjects.

" The narrow limits to which you have reduced your exceptions, and the generality of the affurances you have given of a reftoration of the former conftitutions, were, I doubt not, well confidered and judged neceffary and expedient; *but as there are many things in the conftitutions of fome of the Colonies, and fome things in all, which the people have always wifhed to be altered, and others which the common advantage of both countries required to be changed,* it is neceffary to be attentive that either your acts or declarations preclude any difquifition of fuch fubjects, or prevent fuch alterations being made in their conftitutions, as the people may folicit or confent to. The inftructions tranfmitted to the truftees of rebel eftates in Carolina, appear to be very proper and applicable to the cafe of the Britifh creditors, and thofe to whom I have communicated them, exprefs themfelves well fatisfied with them.

I am, Gentlemen,

Your moft obedient humble fervant.

(Signed)   GEORGE GERMAIN."

" *Commiffioners for reftoring Peace.*"

ANNOTA-

ANNOTATIONS.

" All propositions from Great Britain for a restitution of peace, from Lord North's conciliatory plan to the above extraordinary declaration, have been a series of treacherous arts and designed ambiguity; and no one, but a person of Lord George Germain's ambiguous character, could so peremptorily have decided that the exceptions alluded to in this Declaration were reduced to narrow limits." ' Excepting always such persons who have been instrumental in putting to death any of his Majesty's loyal subjects,' are the words of the Commissioners, when stripped of superfluous expressions, * Are these narrow limits? What description

* *By their Excellencies* Sir Henry Clinton, *Knight of the most Honourable Order of the Bath, General and Commander in Chief of all His Majesty's Forces, within the Colonies lying on the Atlantic Ocean, from Nova Scotia to West Florida, inclusive, &c &c. &c.——And* Mariot Arbuthnot, *Esquire, Vice Admiral of the White, and Commander in Chief of His Majesty's ships and vessels employed in North America, &c. &c.——His Majesty's* Commissioners *for restoring peace to the colonies and plantations in North America, and for granting pardon to such of His Majesty's subjects now in Rebellion, as shall deserve the Royal Mercy, &c*

A DECLARATION.

TO the inhabitants of the British colonies on the continent of North America, now in rebellion, of every rank, order, and denomination; excepting always such persons, who under the usurped forms of trial, have tyrannically and inhumanly been instrumental in executing and putting to death any of His Majesty's loyal subjects.

Great Britain having manifested the sincerity of her affectionate and conciliatory intentions, in removing for ever your pretended grounds of discontent, by repealing among other statutes, those relating to the duty on tea, and the alterations in the government of Massachusett's Bay; and by exempting for ever not only the continental, but the insular colonies, from parliamentary taxations; it is with much pleasure we make known to you, that we have received a commission, under the great seal of Great-Britain, which has for its objects the removal of distrusts by the remission of offences—the restoration of the benefits of an extensive commerce—the enabling the constitutional officers of government to re-assume their functions (that you may again enjoy your former local legislatures) and the confirmation of your rights, liberties, and privileges.

The door is thus again thrown open (if happily you are disposed to avail yourselves of the opportunity it affords) for commencing negociations, which may instantly terminate the miseries of your country.

We do therefore by the authority in us vested, hereby invite all the colonies in rebellion, separately as such, or any associations of men therein, to depute proper persons (for whom on application safe conducts shall be given) to make to us, jointly or separately, or in our absence to our council, (composed of the following members, viz, The Right Honourable Lieutenant

cription of perfons or crimes do they contain? All officers who have given fentence upon courts martial for the condemnation of fpies are fully comprehended ; all judges, juftices, fheriffs, conftables, and other petty

tenant General Charles Earl Cornwallis ; his Excellency James Robertfon, Efquire, Captain General and Governor in Chief of the Province of New-York ; Jofiah Martin, Efquire, Captain General and Governor in Chief of the Province of North Carolina ; William Franklin, Efquire, Captain General and Governor in Chief of the province of New Jerfey ; the Honourable Andrew Elliot, Efquire, Lieutenant Governor of the faid province of New York ; William Smith, Efquire, Chief Juftice of the faid province of New York ; Frederick Smyth, Efquire, Chief Juftice of the faid province of New Jerfey ; and John Tabor Kempe, Efquire, his Majefty's Attorney General of the faid province of New York ; or to the General Officer commanding the King's troops in any of the provinces) all fuch propofitions refpecting the ftate of the faid provinces, modes, or forms of government ; or touching the laws by which they are affected ; and refpecting fuch arrangements and regulations, as may tend to the advantage and ftability of the feveral colonies and provinces, and to a lafting union with each of them refpectively with Great Britain, upon the principles of the conftitution, which his Majefty's fubjects fhall be defirous to confer upon, or lay, through us, before the King, for his royal confideration, and that of his Parliament.

And for the confolation of the friends of peace, and the re-union of the empire, as well as for the encouragement of all who, in future, may adopt the fame fentiments, and by their immediate exertions and example, affift in accomplifhing fo defirable an event ; we declare it to be the intention of Great Britain, by the bleffing of God, to contend for the interefts of the Colonies as infeparably connected with her own, fo that they will neither be left a prey to the rapacious avarice of their domeftic perfecutors, nor to the deep and infidious defigns of their pretended friends and allies.

And while the loyal are exhorted to perfevere in their integrity for the prefervation of their country, its religion and liberties ; we avow to others of every order, who having fo long liftened to the counfels that preferred war to peace, are enabled by their paft experience to decide on the folly of that deftructive choice, our anxious defire for their immediate acceptance of this invitation——As Great Britain in this conteft of arms, ever mindful of your defcent and connection, has fpared what it was, and ftill is in her power to deftroy, and now only wifhes as an affectionate parent, to refcue you from the cruel and tyrannical ufurpations which your leaders are ftruggling to fupport for felfifh and corrupt ends, and at your rifk of being delivered over to Popifh and arbitrary nations.

Having thus announced the benevolent purpofes of our commiffion, We do hereby further declare, to the inhabitants of Pennfylvania, the three Lower Counties on Delaware, New-Jerfey, that part of New York ftill in revolt, Connecticut and Rhode-Ifland, feparately as provinces, or to any affociations of men therein, who fhall on or before the firft day of July next enfuing, declare their abhorrence of the rebellion, feparate from its councils, and afterwards demean themfelves as dutiful and peaceable fubjects of his Majefty's government, that we fhall be ready to grant them pardon for all paft treafons, and the full benefits of the King's clemency as before recited.—We do alfo make the fame offers of pardon and benefits to the inhabitants of the other more fouthern and eaftern colonies in rebellion, or to any affociations of men therein, who fhall on or before the firft day of Auguft next enfuing, declare, and act in the manner aforementioned, and afterwards perfevere in the like-dutiful and loyal behaviour.

If any fhall be fo hardy and defperate as to contemn the proferred clemency of their Sovereign, the liberality of the nation, and the means and mediation we now tender for effecting

petty officers, jurymen, witneffes, and fpectators at the time of execution, may be faid to be inftrumental ' in putting to death his Majefty's loyal fubjects.'

" The word ' inftrumental ' is indefinite. All caufes however re-
mote, which conduce to an event, are ' inftrumental,' and in the
prefent cafe, all thofe who made the laws to enable the judges to
pronounce fentence ; all thofe who elect the legiflators ; all thofe who
contributed, either in the civil or military line, to the revolution have
been ' inftrumental.' [Here followeth feveral expreffions, concerning
the King, which though they have been re-printed by his Majefty's
printer at New-York, might not be permitted with the fame impunity
here.] Thefe, O Britain! are thy terms of proffered mercy to thofe
thou calleft thy deluded children ; calculated for ' the removal of diftrefs
by the remiffion of offences,' and may fucceed when the citizens of
America ceafe to be men ; when the facred love of freedom fhall be
banifhed from the earth, and when heaven fhall ceafe to guard the rights
of mankind! The avowed objects of the commiffion, and which com-
prehend ' too general affurance,' are ' the reftoration of the benefits

affecting the mutual reconciliation of countrymen with each other; and the equitable ad-
juftment and compofure of their differences and ferments ; they are hereby warned of the
aggravation of fuch guilt; and moft earneftly implored to fhun the punifhment ordained by
the laws of their country, and, which, when reftored to their free courfe, will be inflicted
for their treafonable offences.

And that thefe intimations, which fo highly concern the people in the revolted diftricts,
may not be concealed from them to the danger and ruin of any perfon in the future operations, or a tthe final conclufion of the war; We require all officers, civil and military, to be
aiding and affifting with us in the publication thereof, and in the execution of our commiffion,
and of the powers and matters therein contained.

Given under our hands and feals at the City of New-York, this Twenty-ninth day of
December, in the Twenty-firft year of his Majefty's reign.

H. CLINTON,   (L. S.)
Mr. ARBUTHNOT,   (L. S.)

By their Excellencies Command,
DANIEL COXE, p. Secretary.   H

fits of an extensive commerce,' and ' the enabling the constitutional officers of government to reassume their former functions.' A commerce subject to the limitations and restrictions of parliament, and permitted only as a channel through which the fruits of our honest ndustry may be wrested from us to support these ' constitutional officers' in the exercise of their oppressive ' functions.' What might we expect from a restoration of our former local Legislatures? The Minister is undisguised, and directs the Commissioners, that ' neither in their acts nor declarations they preclude disquisitions of subjects which refer to the alteration of former constitutions.' These are alterations ' which the people may solicit or consent to.' By ' people,' we presume his Lordship intends the Tories ' or loyal subjects;' for all others are comprised ' in the limits and exceptions;' and after a sufficient number of them shall be sacrificed to reduce the remainder in a state of abject servility, and despondency, so as to prevent the possibility of future opposition, it would not be difficult to introduce such forms of government as would best suit the purposes of tyranny and oppression.

" Witness the kind of government instituted in Charlestown, under ' the board of police.'

" Philadelphia can declare the wretched fate of the unfortunate citizens of that town. Notwithstanding the most solemn capitulation, by which their persons were to be safe, and their property secured to them, they are inhumanly robbed of all their possessions, driven amongst strangers to seek subsistence for famishing wives and helpless children ! Governor Tonyn in a late speech to the legislature of East Florida, has given a sample of the intended reforms in the colonial governments: His words are, " The result of your deliberations, gentlemen, will not only be of consequence to this province, but to his Majesty's government in general, and will at least give a tincture to future assemblies;

femblies; as one of the chief reafons affigned for this unnatural rebellion in the colonies, refufing to acknowledge the fupreme right and authority of the Britifh parliament, to prevent as far as poffible any future conteft upon fo juft and equitable a point, I hope your good fenfe and attachment to the conftitution will lead you in the moft public and avowed ·manner, by an act of the provincial legiflature, to recognize your allegiance to the bleffed Prince upon the throne, and the ſupremacy of parliament; thereby to eftablifh upon the moft folid foundation, our conftitutional liberties and dependencies.' The obfequious affembly echoed the Governor's fentiments, in the moft fubmiffive language, and have given an example worthy, in his ? ordfhip's opinion, to be followed by the United States. To the feelings of every citizen of America let the appeal be now made. On the one hand, the glorious profpect, is not far diftant, of enjoying in peace and fafety the ineftimable bleffings of civil and political liberty, fecured under the moft excellent conftitutions, formed by themfelves, and fupported, with unfhaken fortitude, through every hazard, and againft every danger.—On the other, a bafe return to the moft barbarous of   with the dreadful though certain expectation of feeling all the effects of Britifh clemency."

Upon the publication of Lord George Germaine's letter by the Congrefs, and fome other letters found in the fame mail, Mr. Jofeph Jones, a delegate in Congrefs from Virginia, wrote in the following terms to Col. Teliefero, an officer in the Virginia camp:

" Some intercepted letters taken in the Falmouth packet for New York, and carried into France and which have been tranfmitted us by our minifter there, clearly fhew the defigns and expectations of the enemy, with refpect to the fubjugation of the Southern States, as well

as

as the continued delufion and folly of the Britifh miniftry; at leaft the
Minifter for the American department, whofe letters we have fo late
as the 5th March, when their then late fucceffes had fo elated them
as to leave no doubt but the Southern States were in fubjection, and
that the fuperior force they had in America would enable Clinton
to fend troops up to the head of Chefapeake; and in conjunction
with the loyalifts of Maryland and Pennfylvania, fubdue thofe States,
and that General Wafhington, commanding but a handful of men,
muft crofs the Hudfon, and take refuge in the Eaftern States; where
being deprived of fuccours and fupplies. from the South, he muft
foon be without men to fupport him, and become a facrifice to
General Clinton's army.—Fair profpect this to Lord George! but
alas! where has it vanifhed? or where did it exift, but in his own
imagination? We are told the Dutch are determined to profecute the.
war, and difpofed to be allied to thefe States. Adieu."*

In the American prints are to be found several other letters from.
different members of the Congrefs, to their friends, reprobating Lord.
George Germain's letter; and ridiculing with no fmall fhare of hu-
mour, a letter from his friend and fecretary, Mr. W. Knox; alfo.
found in the fame packet, and publifhed likewife by the Congrefs; of
which the following is an extract of the only part worthy of notice:
" It is intended to eftablifh amongft them (the Colonies) diftinc-
" tions of rank, and new model their government by that of Great
" Britain."

* This letter was printed in the New York Newfpaper of the 15th of September.
laft.

On the firſt of January 1781, a few weeks before his Lordſhip's letter was written, and probably about the time that it was under conſideration in the *efficient* council, the Congreſs ordered the following army to be in camp,

" Four regiments of Cavalry, 6 troops each, of 64 men,   1536

" Four regiments of Artillery, 9 companies each, of 65 men, — — — —   2340

" Forty-nine regiments of Infantry, 9 companies each, 64 men, — — — —   28224

" One regiment of Artificers, 8 companies each, 60 men, — — — —   480

     32,580

The ſucceſs of the laſt campaign in America, as well as of every other campaign ſince 1775, ought to convince us, that the conqueſt of that vaſt country is hopeleſs ; that the attempt is impracticable ; and that the great promiſes of future ſucceſs, which year after year have been held out to us, and are now made to us for the next year, are like all the paſt, deluſive, irrational and wicked. The nation has been ſeduced by them, year after year, into ruinous expence, and involved, year after year, in additional wars.

During the whole laſt campaign, Sir Henry Clinton was kept at bay, by the menaces of General Waſhington to attack New York. Lord Cornwallis was deprived of ſuccours becauſe Sir Henry Clinton durſt not ſend him any. And at laſt the threatened attack of New York proves to have been nothing more than a feint ; that General Waſhington never intended to attack New York ; but that he affected it, purely to deceive Sir Henry Clinton, and prevent him ſending reinforcements to Lord Cornwallis ; and actually kept him in that ſtate of jeopardy,

I

pardy, until Monfr. de Graffe appeared off the Chefapeak. When that event was known, Sir Henry found, to his great mortification, that he had been *duped*; that Wafhington, fo far from threatening him, had been all the time fecretly laughing at him; and that the huge heaps of letters, which had been taken in the intercepted American mails, ftrongly appeared, to have been written and fent on purpofe, to fall into his hands. But the manœuvre of young Laurens (fon to the ftate prifoner in the Tower) difguifed Mr. Wafhington's movement from before New York, fo effectually, that the true reafon was not fufpected, until fome time after the American chief had begun his march to the Southward, to co-operate with the French Admiral.

This new deception was entrufted to young Laurens, who completely executed it. He circulated a report in Jerfey, in order that it might be conveyed to New York, of circumftances having happened in Europe, which were extremely unfavourable to the French and American interefts. The bait anfwered. In New York it was inftantly credited, and propagated by authority. I fhall give it from the New York Gazette of Auguft 25, * in which it was printed by his Majefty's printer, in a large type (three fizes larger than the other intelligence in the fame paper) to fignify its authenticity and importance.

" A Gentleman, juft arrived from Jerfey, informs us, that young Mr. Laurens, lately pafled through that province on his return from Paris, and has brought the following very interefting intelligence, that the EMPEROR OF GERMANY, HAD DECLARED HIMSELF THE ALLY OF GREAT BRITAIN, [*all in large capitals*], which threw the court of Verfailles into much confufion, as, in confequence of this great event, the French nation muft withdraw all fupport from their new allies the rebels of this continent; and we are informed that it has with another concurring

* Monfr. de Graffe arrived in the Chefapeak on the 26th. of Auguft.

curring circumſtance occaſioned Mr. Waſhington and the Count de
Rochambault to quit their *menacing* poſition at the White Plains, where
we are aſſured the French and rebel troops did not conſort together as
men determined either to ſecure the independence of America, or realize
Mr. Waſhington to be a dictator of it. We are alſo told, that the French
admiral is embarking all the ſick troops on board his ſquadron, from
which it is ſuggeſted that their fleet and army are to be withdrawn from
Rhode Iſland, to ſtrengthen themſelves in the Weſt Indies. It is ſaid
that the French and rebels left their ground the day after Mr. Waſhington received the mortifying account of the Emperor's alliance with his
Majeſty's old and natural friend the court of Great Britain."

Inſtead of the French *coming to* America with a greater force, they
were here repreſented to be *going from* America, with all they had there.
The inference is obvious, viz. that Lord Cornwallis could want no
aſſiſtance !

I do not know whether this ſtratagem of young Laurens, may not
fall heavy upon his father. His Grace of York is in great favour, and
he may adviſe the inverſion of the Moſaic Law ; that is, to viſit the
ſins of the ſon upon the father, to the third and fourth year of impri-
ſonment. As the gallant Earl in Virginia has ſuffered, may it not be in-
ferred that young Laurens certainly was the cauſe of it. It was he who
concluded the deception, practiſed upon Sir Henry Clinton.

Thus hath the American chief, by his artful manœuvres, obliged
us to waſte a whole ſummer upon the defenſive at New York ; and by
his extraordinary ſkill, and having a large ſtage to act upon, has wound
up the campaign, with honour to himſelf, and advantage to his country.
While we have been continued under the immenſe expence, of preſerving a place of arms, from which we could not act, except by one
or two deſultory, or rather marauding expeditions ; of no moment
to the great object of the war ; and of no honour to our national character ;

racter ;—— Mr. Washington with a small army, confeffedly not half of that within New York, has kept Sir Henry Clinton inactive all summer; has prevented him from reinforcing the southern army, or even making a diverfion in favour of it. And at length to wind up the meafure of Britifh calamity and difgrace, has (affifted by that very Rochambault, whom the King's fervants at New York, drove by a fingle dafh of the pen to the Weft Indies) compelled thofe gallant but unfortunate troops, who in all the brilliancy of fuccefs had traverfed South and North Carolina, to furrender to an imprudently defpifed but now victorious enemy.

However, Sir Henry Clinton is a brave officer, and has behaved like one upon every occafion ; and if in fome eyes, he appears to have acted with a judgment inferior to Mr. Washington, it has been owing to the fmallnefs of his theatre, and to the want of a proper regulation at home; where no fyftem was formed, nor plan of operation ever laid down, in which common fenfe could be difcovered. He is obliged to act in every department at New York ; from the commander in chief to the futler.

The two great errors refpecting the conduct of the war, have been, firft a want of true information, or a total difregard of it ; and next, a moft criminal indifference about forming any well digefted fyftem of policy and action, embracing in it the probabilities of European jealoufy. In a word, the minifters have had no PLAN : There have been no coincidence, no co-operation amongft them. The fleet at New York has never been adequate to the fervice. The war has been left to chance : no provifion was made for difafter, nor has any fingle meafure been concerted for adoption, in cafe of victory. When a temporary advantage has been obtained, by the fpirit of the officers, and the innate bravery of the troops, the minifters have always claimed the merit of it. But if the commander has been mifled by falfe information, or overpowered by numbers, the blame is fixed entirely and exclufively upon him : and a party of the American refugees, refident in London, who are paid

for

for defamation, and who by the local knowledge they have of each scene of action, are enabled to torture, mistate and misrepresent his motions, raise from premises of their own, raise arguments and falshoods, which pass uncontradicted. The fair fame, and well-earned reputation of the commander, are wounded and traduced, through all the public prints, in hand-bills, and in pamphlets ; and it is upon strong suspicion, that ministers are charged with giving their assistance, besides countenance and circulation, to this wicked and artful fraud upon the public. The case of Sir William Howe one day, is the case of Sir Henry Clinton another : and it is more than probable, that if General Burgoyne had joined in an attack upon Sir William Howe, he might have been, what Lord Amherst is, or have enjoyed some other post equally as lucrative : ——But this brave and persecuted officer is sensible that Sir William Howe has given the most distinguished proofs of military experience, gallantry and conduct. To these and to his general worth, and humanity, the officers of his army have borne the fullest and most public evidence.

It is needless to assert, that the honour, · principles, and elevated ideas of General Burgoyne, would always incline him to spurn at so infamous and horrid a proceeding as that of attempting to vilify the irreproachable heroism of a fellow soldier. In spite of unexampled accusation and abuse. In spite of glaring insult, intolerable to a mind less conscious of integrity than his own, his character which shines brighter when separated from the professional advantages that were barbarously torn from him, lies far beyond the reach of either the baffled malice of the minister, or the hired calumny, of the refugees.

Our naval power in America, has never been, in any part, what it should have been ; but uniformly insufficient, from the commencement of the war, to the present hour. When D'Estaing arrived on the American coast, it was a miracle, that the fleet, army and New York, were not all taken by him. Nothing but the universal confi-

K

dence

dence in Lord Howe's skill, bravery and general character, prevented so great a fatality. The judicious disposition, which Lord Howe made of his little fleet, awed D'Estaing, and saved the British power in America. If he had not formed that disposition, or had quitted it, he must inevitably have lost the whole ; his force not being half that of the French Admiral. Yet it has been Lord Sandwich's boast, that England never had a better fleet. I will ask, where has it been employed ? or where is it to be found ? Not in the Mediterranean, as the invasion of Minorca shews.— Not in the Baltic, for there we must not fire a gun : it is now the Empress's naval manor and she has forbidden then English shooting there.* ————Not in the channel which was formerly

* The Instrument of our *humble acquiescence* is in these words.

GEORGE R. An additional instruction to all ships of war and privateers, that have or may have, letters of marque against the French King, the King of Spain, or the States General of the united Provinces, their vassals or subjects, or others inhabiting within any of their countries, territories or dominions, or against any other enemies or rebellious subjects of the crown of Great Britain. Given at our court at St. James's, the 20th day of April, 1781, in the 21st year of our reign.

Whereas we have been desirous to prevent interruption being given to the trade and commerce of every state in amity with us as far as was compatible with the necessary operations of war : and whereas it will tend very much to that purpose, that *the trade and navigation of the Baltic should remain uninterrupted*; we have therefore been pleased to resolve, that so long as the trade of our subjects shall continue to be secured in those seas, *our ships of war, privateers and other vessels acting under our commission, shall be restrained from making prize of, stopping, or detaining any ship, or vessels within the Baltic : and we do hereby strictly charge and enjoin the commanders of our ships of war, and the commanders of all ships and vessels, having letters of marque or reprisal, that they do not, by virtue of their commissions, or under colour thereof, stop or detain any ship or vessel in the Baltic,* for the purpose of making prize of the same, but that they suffer all such ships and vessels as they shall meet with in those seas to proceed in their respective voyages, without any interruption. By his Majesty's Command
STORMONT.

merly *our* naval manor, for France, Spain, Holland and even America
now daily and nightly poach in it, and the combined fleets have frequently been masters of it, during which times our game-keeper never
presumed to take their guns : a tacit acknowledgment that our mane-
rial rights are no longer tenable by the law of arms.——— Not in the
West Indies, of which Granada, Tobago, St. Vincent's, and Domi-
nica, are melancholy proofs.——— Not in North America, which the
late engagement off the Chesapeak, and the surrender of the southern army
unquestionably shew.   The French conquer in the West Indies during
the summer, and in the hurricane months, their ships go up to North
America, where they get supplied with fresh provisions, and other ar-
ticles ; and at the same time convoy a great trade to, and from, the
American continent. If our navy is more respectable than ever, what
justification can be given for Admiral Darby's last cruise? Did not
our naval minister know, that the Spanish flota was at that time
on the sea, with an immense treasure ? The combined fleet which
we were not able to face, being returned into port many weeks before,
why was not Admiral Darby ordered to go down, and endeavour to
intercept the flota ? He might have carried relief to Gibraltar at the same
time. It may be now a question, whether we can spare a fleet to relieve
Gibraltar ? Monsieur de Grasse in all human probability is gone to the
West Indies, or Jamaica : he will certainly not stay upon the American
coast at this season and the object of his going there fully answered. A
wise minister would not lose a moment in sending a fleet to the West
Indies. The fleet which sailed a few days ago from Brest is universally
supposed to be gone thither.———If it is true, that we never had a better
fleet, it is also true, that it never was employed to so little purpose.

   The only place in which we have been successful against the French,
has been in Asia ; and that was at the beginning of the war. But the
first Lord of the Admiralty, who is so ready to take merit to himself
upon every little occasion, even upon the capture of a privateer, &c. has

no

no concern in it. All the ministers are perfectly innocent of it. Chandenagore and Pondicherry, were taken by the company's forces; the first in consequence of early information arriving in Bengal, of the delivery of the French rescript in London; which information ministers did not send. The orders for attacking Pondicherry, went from the court of directors, and are dated before the Belle Poule was taken, or any other hostilities had been committed in Europe, between France and England. Matthews carried them over land. He was exactly a month in going from Suez to India. If Pondicherry had not been taken at the critical time it was, it could not have been taken afterwards.*

I know it has been said by the friends of the ministry, that notwithstanding this untoward complexion of things, and notwithstanding we have been awed and insulted in the channel, the inhabitants of the capital, who ought to be the first alarmed upon every occasion, because they are the first informed, did not behold the enemies fleet in the channel in any tremendous light; and even when the combined fleet was off Plymouth, they were indifferent, the diversions and amusements went on, and the people frequented them as usual. The fact is unquestionably true. But it is no proof that danger did not exist; or, that the people did not see it; or, that they did not think the danger very great. The fact is as capable of a different construction, as it is of that which the minister's friends have put upon it. It is as fair to say, that the people seeing every day nothing but a continuation and encrease of oppressive

taxes

* In a week after the surrender, the rains set in; which would have made it impossible for the troops to have kept the field. This success is to be ascribed to a number of fortunate circumstances. First, the orders reaching India in such an extraordinarily expeditious manner. Next, the great activity of the new government of Madras; (Col. Stuart, &c. being recalled) and the new men being extremely alert, to shew their assiduity. Twelve thousand men were in the field by the end of June. The French rescript was laid before the House of Commons on the seventeenth of March, preceding.

taxes, a decrease every year of dominion and trade, are indifferent to any change ; and may think that none can be for the worse : they have been repeatedly promised, what has never been performed : they were promised a revenue from America to ease their burdens ; but their own burdens have encreased, beyond all example in the same number of years, and America is lost ; together with the inestimable riches, and revenue of a flourishing trade. They have paid greater sums for a navy, than ever were known before ; and never had so little benefit from it ; the French alone are able to look it in the face. They were told, that their money was safer in the hands of government, than in any other security ; yet the consolidated stock, which is called the barometer of the funds, is fallen from 90 to 55 ; and land, from being above thirty, is every where below twenty years purchase. The minister is giving every year, eight and nine per cent. for money ; which would be usury in any other man. Can the manufacturer, merchant, or trader borrow money at five per Cent. when the minister annually gives eight, and upwards ?——— No man capable of reflection, can behold these things with indifference ; and if the dread of civil commotion, or the effects of a riot, connived at, if not secretly approved by ministers, prevent him shewing his disapprobation publicly, they equally extinguish his zeal against the common enemy.

The northern princes, who would have crept under their icicles at Lord Chatham's frown, or would shrink to their caves, if Mr. Keppel's and Lord Howe's flags were flying on our fleets, have united in purposes and views, no matter how expressed, or pretended, which are hostile to our interests. Knowing that our resources are not called out ; that our ministers have not the confidence of the people, and consequently not the power to put forth the strength of the nation ; that the force employed is misdirected as to the object ; and that our naval minister has driven from the service the best officers of the fleet ; they venture out of

L   the

the Baltic, which we have complaifantly yielded to their exclufive dominion ; and our enemies obtain, under neutral colours, the moft effential
and conftant affiftance, while their fubjects, unde the fame privilege, and
without rifk, carry on a free and lucrative trade.

The northern confederacy is like a new nation rifing in Europe; a
Phœnix emerging out of the old commercial, enterprifing fpirit of Great
Britain. Mr. Gibbon will perhaps call it, another union of Northern
barbarians, formed to invade and fubdue the effeminate refinements, of
modern Romans. It is certainly a new epoch in the hiftory of Europe ;
and demands all our addrefs, care and attention. The hemifphere thic-
kens wherever we turn our view. The *original* ftatefman ;* the con-
trouling eye of a refponfible fupreme minifter, who will fearch for, and
accept of, information and inftruction in every channel ; who, upon a
hint, would fend a Wood to explore ; had prudence to compare, capacity
to judge, and fpirit to refolve.——— He is wanted in every department.
The lofs is felt more, and greater than ever. The King of Pruffia is
indeed faid to be his own minifter ; but the Britifh cabinet, which affects
to hold out an imitation of that monarch, is, in truth, a moft offenfive
and ridiculous burlefque of him.

The armed neutrality, as it is called, muft be confidered by every
friend to Great Britain as tending, eventually, to create, and in a fhort
time, may eftablifh, a rival to our navigation and flag. This is not a
matter to fleep over, nor to be publicly difcuffed. Your former *difcourfe
on the neutral nations* will be of no ufe upon this occafion. Another
kind of difcourfe, and another fyftem of policy, fhould inftantly be
adopted. But fearing the mifchiefs of future mifconduct, from the
known

* This was one of Lord Chatham's expreffions in the Houfe of Lords, when he re-
probated the fecret influence. He faid, there was no original minifter ; no minifter in
whom meafures could be afcertained to originate, &c.

Known mifchiefs of paft mifcondudt, I think no veracity will be hazarded
in faying, that the prefent minifters are as unequal to any tafk of negotiation, as they have fhewn themfelves unequal to every operation of
war ; and therefore that any meafure, however excellent in the defign,
would, by them, be marr'd in the execution.

The Northern nations have been united by our temerity : they have
been led, by the ignorant hauteur of our minifters, to confider us, in
their cabinets, as their common enemy. The wicked fpirit of domination, which we began to exercife near home, in fupport of that other
wicked fpirit, which had fuggefted the American war, has cemented an
union amongft thofe nations againft us, who never were friends before.
—— See to what length your American madnefs extends ! Thofe powers would never have been united, but to check the impotent infolence
of your falfe pride, and falfe policy which have made every prince in
Europe your enemy, without making any one man your friend.

The effedt which this northern confederacy muft have upon the terms
of peace, whenever they come to be agitated, will probably be of the
utmoft importance. If Ruffia affumes the charadter of mediatrix, to
which it has been publicly faid, fhe has been humiliated by our court ;
will fhe not fecure fomething important for herfelf ? will not Sweden
and Denmark, add their weight to the demands of America ? Bergen is
the moft convenient port in the north fea, for the American trade. America will there get fail duck, canvas, ofnabrugs, hemp and mafts ; and
the northern nations will get her tobacco, indigo, &c. &c. Is it probable, that the King of Denmark will negledt making ufe of this advantage ?
or that America, who has tafted it, will forget it ? or that Sweden will
not fee her advantage alfo, in ftrengthening the American claim to an
open trade ? The more Powers our infanity provokes upon this queftion,
the ftronger we fix the feal to the Independence of America.

Charles-

Charleſtown was taken in May, 1780. From that time to the preſent, our operations in America, have been principally directed to the ſouthern colonies. Lord Cornwallis has marched almoſt through South and North Carolina, and notwithſtanding he defeated the American arms in repeated actions, the vanquiſhed ſeemed to gain ſtrength by their de-feats; for after every victory he had gained, the Americans collected, and were more numerous than before. After two fighting campaigns in the ſouthern colonies, we have gained Charleſtown and loſt Florida; we have exchanged a province for a town. And Lord Cornwallis, after being obliged to abandon his conqueſts, proceeded, by ſea, to Virginia; where he has been obliged to ſurrender. With all the ſtriking peculi-arities of his fate, he has not, like General Burgoyne, been limited to a particular path, or directed to a ſingle object. He has been at liberty to act in what manner, and to go to what place, he pleaſed. Without any of thoſe reſtraints, however, which deſtined General Burgoyne to de-feat, his lordſhip's danger *certainly* appears to have been not leſs. The ſucceſſes of General Burgoyne in the north, and of Lord Cornwallis in the ſouth, are not diſſimilar; they equally encreaſed the ardour, and number, of their enemies: and they ſerve to ſhew, as inconteſtibly as the ſtrongeſt evidence can ſhew, the impoſſibility of our conquering America.

What man can read your plan of naval operations for the year 1782 without the utmoſt contempt of the judgment that framed it and the ame abhorrence of the folly that publiſhed it.* If the enemy is not
pre-

---

* In the London Chronicle of Tueſday November 20th, 1781, printed by William Strahan, Eſqr. member of parliament, and printer to the King's moſt excellent Majeſty, is the following notification.

" *The Naval Arrangements of the enſuing Spring.*

" For the American ſtation—the Admirals Digby and Hood, with 14 or 15 ſail of the line, and three fifties, beſides frigates, ſloops, ſchooners, and cutters. This force to be encreaſed or decreaſed as circumſtances may require.

At

prepared, will he not prepare, to counteract it, in every part? Can Admiral Graves, or Sir George Rodney, be in the West Indies time enough, to prevent any attack that may be intended on Jamaica? will not announcing to the world, the defign of fending thofe officers thither, urge and ftimu-late the enemy, to feize the prefent opportunity, to attack fome of our iflands, before the reinforcements arrive?-----And will not the French and Dutch fend advices to their fettlements in the Eaft Indies, of the force we are preparing to fend there? In poffeffion, as they are, of all the inftructions, which the minifters fent to the Eaft Indies, can it be a doubt, that they are not prepared to oppofe, and fruftrate our defigns there? Has not every word of thofe inftructions been printed in the Mauritius gazette, very lately? By what *fatality*, or rather by what *intrigue* (for I fufpect the laft) did the enemy get poffefsion of thofe valuable papers?

It has been a misfortune to this country, that many well-meaning gentlemen, did not, when the war commenced, underftand the true con-nexion between America and Great Britain. They adopted certain notions of power; which, with refpect to America, would have been found as impolitic in the execution, as they have been impracticable in the attain-

M   ment.

At the Leward Iflands—Sir George Rodney and Admiral Drake, with 26 fail of the line, 16 of which are to be frefh fhips from England, all copper-bottomed, befides a proportionate number of frigates, fire-fhips, bombs, &c.

On the Jamaica ftation—Admiral Graves, who is to go thither from America with fix fhips of the line, immediately after the expected action with the French, to fucceed Admiral Rowley (who now commands there fince Sir Peter Parker came away), who comes home next fpring. His fquadron to be encreafed to eight fail of the line.

In the Eaft Indies—Sir Richard Bickerton is to have 12 fail of the line, fix of which he takes out with him, frefh fhips, all coppered, from England, befides two fifties and four frigates."

On thefe four ftations the number of fhips of the line will be 61 fail.

ment. Trade alone was our proper connexion ; and fo long as the Americans went on with agriculture, and we with manufactures, both countries were flourifhing : and never was any connexion, between nations, fo happily, and by nature fo mutually formed, for each others be—refit. While we fent them ploughfhares, protected their trade, and let alone their internal police, they were our friends. We went on in manufacturing, and they in cultivating. A dear bought experience has fhewn us, the mifchiefs which an interruption of that happinefs has occafioned. The arguments of thofe noblemen and gentlemen, who depricated the vengeance of miniflers, and folicited the confideration of every meafure, to avoid that of war, reflect a luftre upon their characters, and infpire a confidence in their judgments, which time will not tarnifh, or erafe. If a tax of three pence per pound upon tea, was a matter worth refifting, and America could be brought to unite againft that paltry fum, is it not *more* probable, that the *greater* fum intended to have been levied by the ftamp act, would have created the like refiftance ? There was wifdom in forefeeing the danger, and there was virtue in preventing it. If the policy which dictated the repeal of the ftamp act, had been continued, Great Britain and America would, at this day, have been a moft happy, united and flourifhing people. By adhering to that policy in one cafe, and by rejecting it in another, which was exactly fimilar, we have given it a FAIR TRIAL ; and may pronounce, what woeful experience will not now fuffer to Le called adulation, that the fupporters of that policy were the trueft friends to Great Britain ; to that union and reciprocity of interefts, which gave dignity to our fovereign in the eyes of all the princes in Europe ; and magnanimity to our councils, by 'a thorough knowledge of the commercial fountains from which our ftrength and refources flowed.

I will quit this difagreeable and melancholy fubject, with moft earneftly entreating you, as chairman, mafter, head, or principal, of the Efficient Council,

Council, not to make another campaign in America.——— Abandon the American war.——— Say nothing more about it ; but withdraw the troops, and employ them elsewhere. Make no peace with America only. Leave all discussion with America to the period of a general peace. The separate attempt would be degrading ; and would be paying to America a greater compliment than you intend. Follow Lord Chatham's plan ; you cannot follow a better. The House of Bourbon was always his object. We are already engaged in a triple war in Europe ; and know not how soon it may be encreased. To combat the House of Bourbon as we ought, would employ all the strength, riches and resources of the nation. If the house of Bourbon is not essentially weakened, no peace can be made that is not dishonourable, disadvantageous and insecure.

The service you have it in your power to render your country, by changing the present plan of action, may be very well stiled inestimable. A cursory review of measures, during only the last six years, is amply sufficient to convince any gentleman, of the necessity of a total alteration in them. I will hope, that your candour will not allow you to defend them. If we reason upon the probability of the future, from the knowledge we have of the past, which is always a fair presumption, the necessity of changing the system, and principle, at present so prevalent in his Majesty's councils, will be manifest to any understanding. Idiotism itself could not have produced such a series of misfortunes. I will not enumerate them ; nor point out where, I think, owing to either the inattention, or incapacity of ministers, we are exposed to more misfortunes. But as a friend to my country, I wish to see the authors of her calamities removed, and an almost total change made in the measures of government. Lord North is called the ostensible minister, and you, Sir, the real one.

The same wicked spirit of domination, which has lost America, hath also provoked, and excited the Asiatic princes to enter into a league against

us

us. While Hyder Ally alone, has taught them, that our troops are not in-
vincible. We are now going to carry on a continental war there.———Is it
to make our foveroign a Nabob, that the elector of Hanover's troops are
tranfporting to Afia ? or, are they intended, to add to his dominions, the
empire of the Eaft, becaufe his minifters have loft that of the Weft ?—
Notwithftanding fo many deferving naval officers are unemployed, whom
the breath of flander never touched, yet captain Sir Richard Bickerton,
junior to all of them, is to have the command. This officer cannot be
injured by faying, there are many more proper for it ; ——— but as the
official minifters are the dependents of the efficient council, fo the officers,
they employ, muft be the dependents of the official minifters. Since
America has become independent, they are afraid of every thing, that is
fuppofed to bear the moft diftant analogy to it. It would be prudent,
however, before you precipitate the nation into a continental war in Afia
——— to reflect a little ——— to look round for advice. A continental war
in Afia may prove as fatal to our fettlements there, as the continental war
in America has been. I am no party man in oriental politics. Great
advantages, under wife regulations, may be derived from the Eaft. I
remember Lord Chatham called it, the rifing fun of the Britifh empire.
But I believe he would never have thought of fending a body of Hano-
verians thither. A new fyftem is wanted for that country ; the prefent
is impolitic and ruinous. There are men, now in England, who ought
to be confulted upon that meafure. Mr. Francis, claims the earlieft attention ; not more for his clear, quick and intelligent conception ; his
general and indifputable knowledge of all the *prefent* circumftances of
the Eaft ; than for his penetration and good fenfe, upon all occafions :
and next to him, is, the author of the *Origin and Authentic Narrative
of the Marratta*, and *Rohilla wars*. Lord Chatham fearched for ; and
obtained, from gentlemen of their upright fairnefs and candour, thofe
pure fountains of truth, from whence ftreamed the fuccefs of his meafures.

Thofe

Thofe perfons who have thought that the war with America was a right meafure, muft admit, that the Minifters have fhewn a total want of capacity in the manner they have carried it on. If the plan was right at Bofton, it was wrong to go to New-York. Every fucceeding year has been made to contradict and condemn the preceding. The conclufion from which is, that the Minifters are not capable of conducting a war; that they are incompetent to the tafk; but their ready and implicit acquiefcence in all the impolitic meafures and extravagant projects of the Efficient Council fecures their continuance in office. If the Efficient Council could have accomplifhed a change of men,* and at the fame time have preferved their own exiftence and power, a change of Minifters would have taken place fome time ago. Nor have there been wanting feveral attempts, with the principal characters in oppofition, and fome very lately, to affect this purpofe; but, however fpecious the arguments made ufe of, and however tempting the allurements held out, nor however flandered with a craving for places; yet, no arguments could perfuade, no allurements feduce, no flanders provoke, the friends of their country to defert that duty, they have uniformly held facred to their fellow fubjects. However honourable every honeft mind muft think it to ferve his country, as foon could Mr. Keppel or Lord Howe truft themfelves under Lord Sandwich, as the Marquis of Rockingham or the Earl of Shelburne under the Efficient Council.

When we behold the Duke of Richmond, fo highly honoured by, and fo well deferving the confidence of his country,

The Duke of Grafton, who felt the weight of that fecret influence in precipitating the nation into a civil war, which it was his moft anxious wifh to prevent,

N

The

---

* The Lord Advocate of Scotland knows his own affair with the Right Honourable Welbore Ellis.

The Marquis of Rockingham, to whofe merits and fervices in he public caufe, all words would be but a faint tribute of acknow-edgement and gratitude,

The Earl of Shelburne, (the difciple of Lord Chatham) fitted by nature, by habit, and experience, for the government of an empire,

Lord Camden,

———— When he fpeaks,
The air, a charter'd libertine, is ftill,
And the mute wonder lurketh in men's ears,
And fteals his fweet, and honied fentences !

Together with many more ; and a long train of illuftrious Commoners, not inferior to them in ability, and zeal for their country ; whofe high characters and talents have gained them the applaufe and veneration of all good men,—Can it be a matter of furprize to any Englifhman, tha the nation is diffatisfied at their not being in the public fervice ? The nation has a claim to the abilities of fuch men ; they are, if I may be allowed the expreffion, a fort of public property; but how greatly muft our diffatisfaction encreafe, and our indignation be excited, if we contraft them with the oftenfible minifters, fuch as, Lord North, Lord Sandwich, Lord Stormont, Lord Hillfborough, Lord George Germain, &c. in whofe hands the empire is crumbling. to atoms, is difhonoured at home, difmembered abroad, and in-fulted every where ?

Lord Bacon fays,* " It is in vain for Princes to take counfel
" concerning matters, if they take no counfel concerning perfons ;
" for all matters are as dead images, and the life of the execution of
" affairs refteth in the advice of good perfons. Neither is it enough
" to confult concerning perfons *fecundum genera,* as an idea of ma-
" thematical

* In his Effay of Counfel.

" thematical defcription, what the kind and character of the per-
" fon fhould be; for the greateft errors are committed, and the
" moft judgment is fhewn in the choice of individuals."

I will now take my leave of you, Sir, with a fhort admonition
and recommendation. We have feen in thefe pages proofs fufficient, of the unconftitutional authority of, and the mifchiefs occafioned by, the *efficient council*; and of the fervile acquiefcence, and
total incapacity of the *official minifters*. An increafe of our misfortunes, muft in a fhort period prove fatal to both. The community
cannot bear oppreffion and difafter, with a furrounding profpect of defpair, while the fame men govern, without calling for the authors of
their calamities. Seize, therefore, the opportunity, which the prefent
hour of fufpence affords, to abolifh the firft, and difmifs the fecond.
When thefe men are no longer in fight, hope may arife: from other
hands we may expect different meafures; and the public ftrength will
gain new vigour, by a reftoration of loft confidence. Upon an
appointment of able men to the great departments in the State, there
would inftantly blaze a new fpirit to retrieve the honour of this
country. That cloud of indifference and defpondency, with which it
is at prefent overcaft, would inftantly difappear. Confidence in the
minifters, would enfure fuccefs to the exertions of the people.

I am, S I R,

Your moft humble fervant,

Nov. 26, 1781.

An Independent Whig.

www.ingramcontent.com/pod-product-compliance
Lightning Source LLC
Chambersburg PA
CBHW030903260626
47169CB00008B/2666